DEVILCHILD

VOLUME I: HELL IS ROUND THE CORNER

By
Andy Winter
&
Natalie Sandells

with
PeeT!
Tim Doe
Tim Twelves

To Julie
Nice to meet
you at last!

To Julie,
Have a
devilishly
good festival.
all the best.

Moonface Press

DEVILCHILD VOLUME I: HELL IS ROUND THE CORNER

Published by Andy Winter (Moonface Press)
P.O. Box 5593
Southend-on-Sea
Essex
UK
SS1 2WY

Printed in the UK by The Book Factory

Visit our website at: www.devil-child.co.uk

ISBN 0-9542739-0-7

Contents

Devilchild

Written and lettered by Andy Winter
Illustrated by Natalie Sandells

7

Velocity Girl

Written by Andy Winter
Illustrated and lettered by Tim Twelves

64

Feathers

Written by Andy Winter
Illustrated by Tim Doe

71

Dosh & Pecs Do Time Travel

Written and lettered by Andy Winter
Illustrated by PeeT!

80

For Bill and Kurt

HELL IS ROUND THE CORNER
writer/letterer: Andy Winter artist: Natalie Sandells
UNDERWORLD
UNDER WORLD
...HAPPY BIRTHDAY DEAR TROY, HAPPY BIRTHDAY TO YOOOUUU...

10

CHRIST, WHAT A WAY TO SPEND MY BIRTHDAY. GETTING ...HFFF... CHASED DOWN CAMDEN HIGH STREET BY A... A... WHAT WAS THAT ...WHFFF... THING ANYWAY?

MARILYN MANSON'S PLAYING IN TOWN TONIGHT. THAT DAFT BUGGER BRINGS THE FREAKS OUT IN DROVES.

YEAH, BUT THE ...WHHFF... ONE WHOSE HAT FELL OFF HAD GREEN SKIN, RED EYES AND THESE BIG ...WHFFF... FUCKING TEETH!

GREEN SKIN, MY ARSE! YOU'VE BEEN OVERDOING IT ON THE SKUNK AGAIN, HAVEN'T YOU TROY-BOY?

IT'S A GOOD JOB WE'VE LOST THEM, COZ YOU DON'T LOOK LIKE YOU COULD RUN ANOTHER STEP!

...HHRRFF... WHAT DO YOU... ...WHFF... THINK A PANCREAS LOOKS LIKE, B?

I'M SURE I HAVE NO IDEA.

ONLY I THINK ...HACK... I'VE JUST COUGHED MINE UP!

HANG ON A MINUTE, WHAT HAPPENED TO LUCIA?

YOU DON'T HAVE TO WORRY ABOUT LUCIA...

WHOO! LOOK AT THE TROY BOY! CLEAN SLEATER-KINNEY T-SHIRT, NEWLY-WASHED AND FRESHLY TOUSLED HAIR. JESUS, HE'S EVEN HAD A SHAVE!

♪ ON THE PULL, ON THE PULL, ON THE PULL! ♪

SAYS THE WOMAN WEARING AN ARMANI DRESS AND BRAND NEW BLAHNIKS JUST TO SEE A BAND AT THE CAMDEN UNDERWORLD!

AND, PRAY TELL, WHICH BUNCH OF TONE DEAF PUBLIC SCHOOLBOYS ARE WE CHECKING OUT TONIGHT THEN, TROY BOY?

THEY'RE CALLED CLICHÉ GUEVARA™

AH YES, THE BAD-ASSED GANGSTA RAP/NU-METAL POSSE FROM THE MEAN STREETS OF LEIGH-ON-SEA!

YOU MUSIC JOURNALISTS ARE ALL THE SAME - TOTALLY BLOODY CYNICAL!

Prrp!

I'D RATHER BLOW PRINCE PHILLIP THAN HEAR YOU TWO DRONE ON ABOUT MUSIC, SO CAN WE GO NOW...

PLEASE?!

I'M GOING, I'M GOING!

YOU REALLY DON'T HAVE TO WORRY, YOU KNOW...

"I CAN *SMELL* TROUBLE FROM A *MILE* AWAY."

The *spell* of concealment has been *cast*. The boy will be in *hell* before his so-called *protectors* even realise he's *gone*.

I *hope* you're right Dragonel, or the master will *tear* out our entrails and *use* them as piano wire. Hee hee hee...

What? I'm *only* saying...

SNIFF! SNIFF!

He's on *his* way.

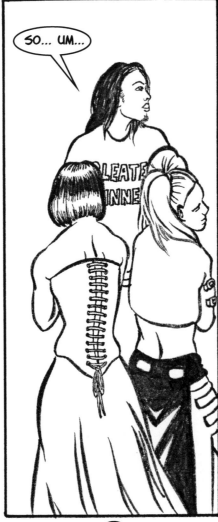

...WE'RE GOING TO NEED SOME HEAVY DUTY *HELP.*

SO, ER, HOW IS THE *ALMIGHTY* THESE DAYS, MICHAEL?

NOT GOOD BEATRICE, NOT GOOD.

THAT WHOLE *OMNIPOTENCE* THING AGAIN?

I'M *AFRAID* SO — HIS CONCENTRATION *DESERTS* HIM ALL THE TIME.

HE EVEN *MISSED* HIS WEEKLY, ER, 'JAM SESSION' THIS MORNING...

...MS *NICO* AND MR *RAMONE* WERE SO *DISAPPOINTED.*

FOR ANY OF YOU WHO MIGHT HAVE *MISSED* THE NEWS FLASH...

...TROY HAS BEEN *SNATCHED* BY A BUNCH OF *DEMONS,*

AND WE'VE BEEN SAT HERE FOR *OVER* AN HOUR *WAITING* FOR THE ALMIGHTY TO GET OFF HIS ARSE AND *HELP* US DO SOMETHING ABOUT IT.

HOW

DARE

YOU?!

CREATOR, DEMONS HAVE *TAKEN* TROY AND...

47 PEOPLE HAVE JUST BEEN KILLED IN A FLASHFLOOD IN INDIA...

OH NO.

...AN UNEMPLOYED WOMAN HAS WON $35 MILLION IN THE LOUISIANA STATE LOTTERY...

ER, CREATOR, DID *YOU* HEAR WHAT I SAID?

...AND THE PENSIONER WHO LIVES NEXT DOOR TO YOU AND LUCIA IS HAVING SEX WITH HIS DOG... AGAIN.

SNAP OUT OF IT, YOU SILLY OLD BUGGER, THIS IS *SERIOUS!*

MY, THAT POOR DOG...

HE'S HAVING ONE OF HIS *'EPISODES',* I'M AFRAID. YOU WON'T GET ANY MORE *SENSE* OUT OF HIM NOW.

...TWO MORE DEAD IN THE LATEST US BOMBING RAIDS ON IRAQ...

WELL, IF YOU TWO *DORKS* AND THE ARTIST FORMERLY KNOWN AS *GOD* WON'T DO *ANYTHING* TO HELP US SAVE TROY...

...WE'LL DO IT OURSELVES. COME ON, B, WE'RE *LEAVING*...

NO, LUCIA, I ABSOLUTELY *FORBID* IT. THERE ARE *DIPLOMATIC* CHANNELS THAT MUST BE *OBSERVED*...

...ANY SORTIE INTO HELL WILL BE SEEN AS AN ACT OF EXTREME *AGGRESSION*...

...YOU COULD START A *WAR!*

...THE JAPANESE PRIME MINISTER HAS JUST BROKEN HIS HIGH SCORE ON TEKKEN...

...A FIVE YEAR OLD BOY SWEPT OUT TO SEA AND DROWNED IN SYDNEY...

THANKS FOR *NOTHING* RAPHAEL, SEE YOU AROUND.

SO *WHAT* DO WE DO NOW? WHIP OUT A ROAD ATLAS AND *LOOK* UNDER 'H' FOR *HELL?*

NOT EXACTLY. I HAVE AN *IDEA.*

NOT HER, B. TELL ME IT'S NOT HER!

CAN'T YOU EXCUSE HER *ECCENTRICITIES* JUST THIS ONCE?

ECCENTRICITIES? THE WOMAN'S A BLOODY LUNATIC!

SHE *TURNS* HER EX-BOYFRIENDS INTO *CATS* AND DRINKS HER OWN *PISS!*

AND *WHAT* ABOUT THAT DEMON SHE *SHAGGED* TO *DEATH* LAST YEAR?

AT LEAST HE DIED WITH A *SMILE* ON HIS FACE!

BESIDES, THE WAY THINGS ARE GOING, SHE COULD BE OUR *ONLY CHANCE* OF GETTING TROY BACK!

RHEA

WITCH ASTROLOGER SEXUAL DEVIANT

TYPICAL! OLD WHITE BEARD UPSTAIRS HAS IT OFF WITH A BEAUTIFUL *VIRGIN*, WHO THEN GIVES BIRTH TO THE *CHRIST* CHILD.

JC PERFORMS *MIRACLES* AND *SACRIFICES* HIMSELF TO SAVE THAT ROTTEN BUNCH OF *BASTARDS* CALLED HUMANITY FROM THEMSELVES...

I, ON THE OTHER HAND, *NAIL* SOME OLD *SLAPPER* IN AN *ALLEY* BEHIND A NIGHTCLUB...

...AND *MY* SON TURNS OUT TO BE A *SNIVELLING* WRETCH WHO *SOILS* HIMSELF THE *FIRST* TIME HE MEETS HIS *OLD MAN!*

GAH! I HAVEN'T BEEN THIS UPSET SINCE I SAW '*BEDAZZLED*'.

LIZ HURLEY PLAYING *ME!?* THE SHEER BLOODY CHEEK OF IT!

On your **feet** whelp, or Guttlehog will **have** your **eyes**.

RETURN TROY TO HIS QUARTERS AND *LEAVE* ME ALONE WITH MY THOUGHTS...

SORRY TO CALL ON YOU SO LATE, RHEA. IT'S TROY, HE'S BEEN *TAKEN*.

WE *NEED* TO TRAVEL TO *HELL* TO GET HIM BACK.

I KNEW THIS WAS A *WASTE* OF TIME. SHE *CAN'T* HELP US!

WITH THE AMOUNT OF *RUTTING* AND *DRINKING* YOU GIRLS DO YOU'LL BE IN HELL SOON ENOUGH, WITHOUT *ANY* HELP FROM ME!

GET YOURSELF A SENSE OF *HUMOUR*, GRUMPY BOOTS, OF COURSE WITCH RHEA CAN *HELP* YOU.

ER, THANKS FOR THE *OFFER*, BUT WE'RE ACTUALLY PRETTY *ANXIOUS* ABOUT TROY.

SO, THE DEVIL CHILD HAS FINALLY BEEN *LOCATED* BY HIS DEAR OLD PAPA, HAS HE? GIVE ME A MINUTE TO FIND MY *BOOK OF SHADOWS* AND WE'LL BE IN BUSINESS.

WHILE YOU'RE *WAITING*, THERE'S AN ABSOLUTE *FUCK-FEST* GOING ON IN THE MASTER BEDROOM... IF YOU'D LIKE TO *PARTAKE*?

OKAY, SUIT YOURSELF, BUT ME AND A COUPLE OF GIRLS FROM THE *COVEN* HAVE *SUMMONED* THIS DEMON WITH A 12-INCH *TONGUE* AND *THREE COCKS*, WE...

LA, LA, LA, LA, WE'RE *NOT* LISTENING!

TSSCHH, YOU ANGELS CAN BE SUCH PRUDES!

I **REALLY** WISH YOU'D COME OUT FROM **BEHIND** THE **SOFA**, MY BOY. THE **LAST** THING I WANTED WAS TO **SCARE** YOU.

THIS MUST BE VERY **HARD** FOR YOU, BUT I HAVE TO SAY I'M **AMAZED** IF YOU NEVER **SUSPECTED** THAT YOU WERE, WELL, **DIFFERENT**.

DIFFERENT? IF YOU'RE MY DAD, **DIFFERENT** DOESN'T EVEN BEGIN TO **COVER** IT!

AH, AT **LAST** HE FINDS A **VOICE.** BUT TELL ME, HAVE YOU NEVER THOUGHT YOUR **LIFE** A LITTLE **STRANGE,** TROY?

I **DON'T** KNOW WHAT YOU **MEAN**.

YOU DON'T FIND IT **ODD** THAT TWO **GORGEOUS** YOUNG GIRLS HAVE BEEN YOUR **BEST** FRIENDS SINCE THE DAY YOU TURNED FIVE, AND **RARELY** LEAVE YOUR SIDE?

OR THE FACT YOU **CAN'T** KEEP A PET BECAUSE **NO** ANIMAL WILL **EVER** COME **WITHIN** 20-FEET OF YOU?

OR HOW **EVERY** ENQUIRY YOU'VE EVER MADE ABOUT YOUR **REAL** PARENTS HAS HIT A **BRICK WALL?** AND WHAT ABOUT...

WHAT IS IT THAT YOU'RE SAYING **EXACTLY?**

I'LL **SPELL** IT OUT FOR YOU, **SHALL I?**

YOU WERE **SNATCHED** FROM YOUR MOTHER AT **BIRTH** BY MEMBERS OF HEAVEN'S **SECRET SERVICE.**

BEATRICE AND LUCIA, TWO **WARRIOR** ANGELS, WERE SENT TO BE YOUR **PROTECTORS,** WHILE A **POWERFUL** SPELL KEPT YOU HIDDEN FROM EVEN MY MOST PRODIGIOUS **SORCERERS.**

I'VE SPENT THE LAST 21 YEARS TRYING TO **FIND** YOU!

YEAH, YEAH, BEATRICE AND LUCIA ARE WARRIOR ANGELS AND I'M *RUMPEL-FRIGGIN'-STILTSKIN!*

SO, NOW, WHILE I STILL HAVE A FEW *SHREDS* OF DIGNITY LEFT, CAN YOU JUST SHOW ME THE HIDDEN TV CAMERAS AND GIGGLING STUDIO AUDIENCE, PLEASE?

BEHIND HERE? COME ON, *WHERE* ARE THEY?

AND, WHILE WE'RE ABOUT IT, *WHO* ARE YOU, AND WHICH OF MY SO-CALLED MATES PUT YOU UP TO *THIS?*

I MEAN IT. I *WANT* TO KNOW WHO YOU ARE.

COME ON, TROY, *THINK* ABOUT IT.

FIVE LETTERS: ANAGRAM OF *'SANTA'...*

...LOOKS AND ACTS *NOTHING* LIKE *LIZ HURLEY.*

AH, THE PENNY *DROPS.*

YOU *DISAPPOINT* ME. WHY REMAIN A HUMBLE WAITER, *KISSING* THE PALLID WHITE ARSES OF BANKERS AND ESTATE AGENTS WHEN YOU COULD BE *HERE* AT MY *SIDE?*

WITH THE *POWER* THAT'S IN YOU, YOU COULD HAVE ANY BANKER OR ESTATE AGENT FOR *BREAKFAST*...

...AND I'M *NOT* TALKING *METAPHORICALLY!*

BUT WHY AM I SO *IMPORTANT* TO YOU? *SURELY* YOU HAVE OTHER *CHILDREN?*

ALAS NOT. BELIEVE ME, AFTER YOU WERE TAKEN I *WORKED* MY JOHN THOMAS DOWN TO A *NUB* TRYING TO SIRE ANOTHER *CHILD.*

BUT THAT *ROTTEN* OLD CUNT UPSTAIRS WAS ALWAYS THERE TO PISS ON MY CHIPS — *CAUSING* THE VESSELS OF MY SEED TO *MISCARRY*, TO BECOME *INFERTILE*, TO MEET WITH *'UNFORTUNATE'* ACCIDENTS BEFORE THEY COULD GIVE BIRTH.

I STOPPED TRYING AFTER THE *TWENTY-SEVENTH* TIME.

YOU'RE *TELLING* ME THAT GOD *KILLED* HUMAN WOMEN TO PREVENT YOU *SIRING* AN HEIR?

BLESS YOUR WIDE-EYED *NAIVETE*, MY BOY! HE MIGHT BE A DROOLING OLD *LOONY* NOW, BUT THE ALMIGHTY HAS A MEAN STREAK WIDER THAN THE *GRAND CANYON*, AND MAKES *CALIGULA* LOOK LIKE *EDDIE IZZARD!*

AND, OF COURSE, HE'S *NEVER* FORGIVEN *ME* FOR ALL THAT *'TRYING TO TAKE OVER HEAVEN'* STUFF. *TALK* ABOUT HOLDING A *GRUDGE!*

SO, WHAT DO YOU SAY? LIFE *DOWN* HERE WITH YOUR DEAR OLD *DAD*, DOING WHATEVER AND WHOMEVER YOUR HEART DESIRES?

OR LIFE UP TOP, SERVING *LOBSTER THERMIDOR* TO PRICKS IN SUITS WITH EXPENSE ACCOUNTS?

"THE CHOICE IS YOURS."

THAT BOLLOCK-BREATHED BASTARD RECKONS HE'S GOING TO BITE MY TITS OFF!

YOU TWO CAN LEG IT, IF YOU LIKE, BUT I'M GOING TO KICK THE FUCKER'S HEAD IN!

FOR ONCE IN YOUR LIFE, LUCIA, JUST DO AS YOU'RE TOLD.

NOW, MOVE IT!

I NEVER RUN FROM A FIGHT, B. YOU KNOW THAT.

WHICH IS PRECISELY WHY YOU'LL BE HEADING BACK TO EARTH IN A BODY BAG, IF YOU'RE NOT CAREFUL!

HELL IS QUITE BAD ENOUGH WITHOUT YOU TWO BICKERING LIKE SCHOOL GIRLS!

NOW, TROY'S FATHER IS LIKELY TO BE HOLDING THE BOY AT HIS CHAMBERS IN DIS CITY - THAT'S IT A FEW MILES IN THE DISTANCE.

HOW QUICKLY CAN WE GET TH...

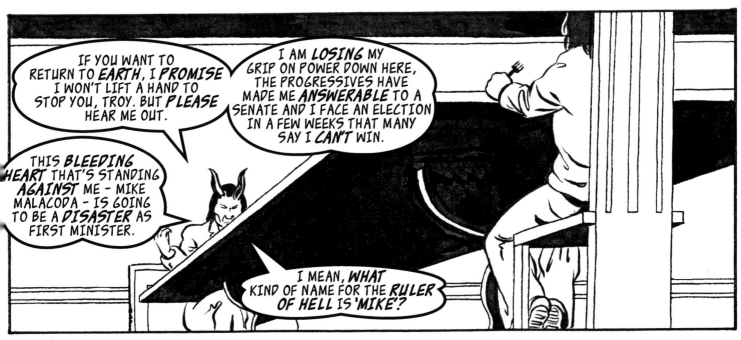

IF YOU WANT TO RETURN TO *EARTH*, I *PROMISE* I WON'T LIFT A HAND TO STOP YOU, TROY. BUT *PLEASE* HEAR ME OUT.

I AM *LOSING* MY GRIP ON POWER DOWN HERE, THE PROGRESSIVES HAVE MADE ME *ANSWERABLE* TO A SENATE AND I FACE AN ELECTION IN A FEW WEEKS THAT MANY SAY I *CAN'T* WIN.

THIS *BLEEDING HEART* THAT'S STANDING *AGAINST* ME — MIKE MALACODA — IS GOING TO BE A *DISASTER* AS FIRST MINISTER.

I MEAN, *WHAT* KIND OF NAME FOR THE *RULER OF HELL* IS 'MIKE'?

PEOPLE ARE GOING TO *SELL* THEIR *SOULS* TO 'MIKE'.

GET THEE *BEHIND* ME, 'MIKE'.

BETWEEN 'MIKE' AND THE DEEP BLUE SEA.

'MIKE' MAKES *WORK* FOR IDLE HANDS.

SYMPATHY FOR 'MIKE'.

IT'S ABSURD!

THEN WHY DON'T YOU JUST WAIT FOR THIS MIKE GEEZER TO *SCREW* IT ALL UP? I BET THEY'LL BE BEGGING YOU TO TAKE CHARGE AGAIN!

CAN'T WAIT AROUND, MY BOY. I WAS *TERRIBLY INJURED* IN HELL'S *GREAT WAR* AND, ALTHOUGH MY *PHYSICIANS* DAREN'T TELL ME TO MY FACE, I SEE *EVERYTHING* I NEED TO KNOW IN THEIR *EYES*...

I'M RATHER *AFRAID* I'M GOING TO *SNUFF IT*, MY BOY.

WHICH IS WHY I NEED YOU TO STAY, *DISCOVER* WHO YOU *TRULY* ARE AND ONE DAY *RULE THE INFERNO* IN MY STEAD.

COOOEEE, ANYBODY HOME?

WHO *DARES* ATTACK ME IN THIS *CRAVEN* FASHION?

MALACODA? NO, I *DON'T* BELIEVE IT — *YOU?!*

WELL, IF IT ISN'T 'STAN, STAN, THE *DEVIL MAN'!*

WE'VE COME TO *COLLECT* OUR FRIEND, STAN, DON'T EVEN *THINK* ABOUT *PISSING* US OFF FURTHER.

REPUBLICAN GUARD, TO MY SIDE!

Already here, master. We came as soon as we heard the <u>tumult</u>.

I've <u>never</u> had the chance to <u>torture</u> and <u>kill</u> a real, live angel before. It's made me quite <u>moist!</u>

I *say* we <u>tear</u> off their wings and <u>piss</u> in the holes!

FIST FUCK THEIR EVERY ORIFICE!

Bite off their tits! Bite of their tits! Hee hee hee.

HEY, I'M *STANDING* RIGHT HERE, YOU KNOW!

WHAT IS IT WITH YOU *FREAKS* DOWN HERE AND ALL THIS *TITTY* BITING?

BELIEVE ME, THERE WILL BE *NO* BITING OF *ANYONE'S* TITTIES, NOT EVEN LUCIA'S — AND SHE *REALLY* LIKES IT!

49

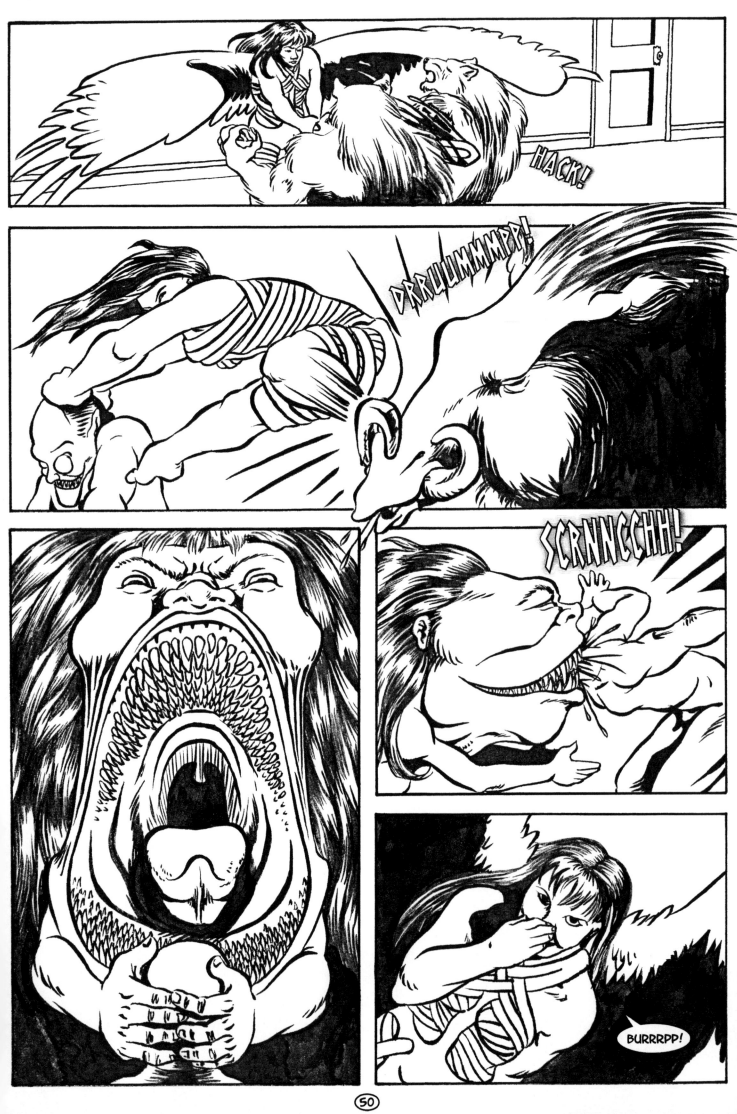

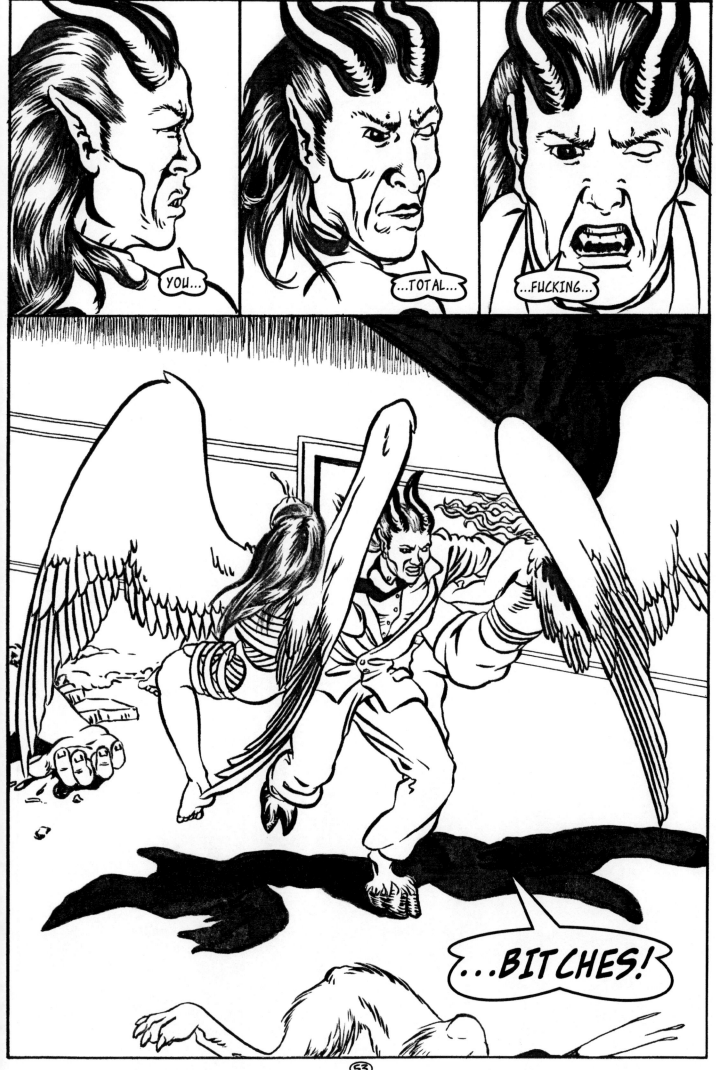

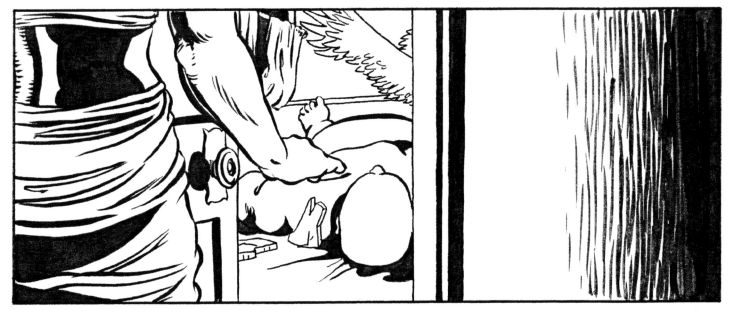

TROY, YOU HAVE TO *STOP HIDING* AND *TALK* TO ME.

WHAM!

"YOUR *FATHER* AND THE *ANGELS* ARE GOING TO *KILL* EACH OTHER, BUT *YOU* CAN *STOP* THEM."

COME ON, BOY, YOU *HAVE* TO LISTEN TO ME. YOU HAVE *GREAT* POWER.

SNAP OUT OF IT!

"POWER ENOUGH TO MAKE THIS *STOP*."

BEATRICE AND LUCIA ARE *DYING* HERE, AND YOU'RE *PISSING YOUR PANTS* LIKE A FIVE-YEAR-OLD.

THEY'RE DYING.

DYING!

SLAP!

THAP!

PRUNK!

AAHHH!

BOOF!

DUFF!

COME ON, B, THIS IS THE *LAST* CHANCE WE'RE GOING TO GET TO *FINISH* HIM, SO LET'S GIVE IT EVERYTHING WE'VE GOT!

KRAAM!

WELL *PLAYED*, GIRLIES, I HAVEN'T HAD A WORK OUT LIKE THIS IN YEARS.

AND TO SHOW MY *APPRECIATION* OF YOUR EFFORTS, I PROMISE YOUR *DEATHS* WILL BE *QUICK*...

WELL, *QUICK-ISH*...

THAT'S *ENOUGH*, FATHER!

T-TROY?

THAT'S MY BOY!

THIS IS A *MARVELOUS* TURN OF EVENTS. *BRAVO* FOR TROY!

SO, LET ME GUESS, YOU'RE READY TO PUT YOUR PAST LIFE *BEHIND* YOU, GET IN TOUCH WITH YOUR *BAD SELF* AND ONE DAY BECOME *RULER OF HELL?*

BY THE WAY, WHO'S THE *UGLY* OLD HUMAN SOW? YOU CAN FIND YOURSELF A *DEMON* GIRL NOW.

DID YOU KNOW SOME OF THEM HAVE *SIX TITS?*

I'M *LEAVING* AND WHAT'S LEFT OF BEATRICE AND LUCIA IS COMING WITH ME.

IF *YOU* OR ANY OF YOUR *PATHETIC* MINIONS MAKE ANY ATTEMPT TO STOP ME, I SHALL TAKE HELL *APART* BIT BY *STINKING* BIT AND HAND THE REMAINS TO *MALACODA* – RIGHT AFTER I TELL HIM THAT I'M YOUR *SON* AND THAT *YOU* ARE *RESPONSIBLE* FOR BRINGING ME HERE.

I'M *SURE* THAT WOULD DO YOUR *ELECTION* CHANCES THE POWER OF *GOOD!*

EPILOGUE

IN *FOOTBALL*, IT WAS A BAD NIGHT FOR THE DIS CITY DYNAMOS. THEY LOST THEIR HELL CUP SEMI-FINAL AGAINST ANTENORA UNITED 2-1, A RESULT WHICH INCREASES PRESSURE ON *COACH DON REVIE*. AND NOW WE RETURN YOU TO OUR MAIN NEWS STORY...

FIRST MINISTER SATAN'S RATING IN OPINION POLLS HAS *SOARED* BY 30 PER CENT, MAKING HIM CLEAR *FAVOURITE* TO WIN NEXT MONTH'S *ELECTION*. THIS UNPRECEDENTED RISE IN POPULARITY COMES JUST HOURS AFTER HELL'S RULER HELPED REPEL AN *ATTACK* ON DIS CITY'S PARLIAMENT BUILDING BY A ROGUE ANGEL CELL SAID TO BE ALIGNED WITH THE *TERRORIST* CHERUBIM ARMY.

THE *ATTACK* CLAIMED THE LIVES OF ALL FIVE MEMBERS OF SATAN'S REPUBLICAN GUARD AND, ALTHOUGH BADLY *INJURED* HIMSELF, THE FIRST MINISTER *STILL* FOUND TIME TO TALK TO HELLTV'S LAVINIA ASDENTE...

...*STRONG* LEADERSHIP... *WAR ON TERRORISM*... A RAFT OF NEW MEASURES... *MALACODA* WEAK AND INEXPERIENCED...

THE END

DEVILISH GREETINGS

Moonface Press, P.O. Box 5593, Southend-on-Sea, Essex, UK SS1 2WY
moonfacepress@hotmail.com

Hello and welcome to volume one of **Devilchild**, the first release from **Moonface Press**.

We're a brand new small-press publisher planning to specialise in original graphic novels. We operate on a shoestring, with any money recouped on this first release finding its way not in to my pocket or even that of the artists, but back into the pot to fund future projects. In other words, at this stage we're poor but genuinely excited about what we've created so far and might go on to create in future.

Which brings us to **Devilchild**, the story of a part-time waiter/rock musician, who discovers that everything he thought he knew about his simple existence is totally, utterly, earth-shatteringly wrong. Suffice to say, Troy (the **Devilchild** of our title) is left with quite a lot to ponder after the events depicted in this first episode. Not only does he look like a CGI effect, but his relationship with secretive flatmates Lucia and Beatrice has been changed forever, and maybe not for the best. Then, of course, there's the small matter of what happens now he's finally discovered the identity of his long-lost, brimstone-scented dad!

In other words, the poor boy's just found himself the strangest extended family in existence - two warrior angels, a permanently horny witch and, of course, the big fella with the horns, hooves and heavy drinking habit. It's the kind of scenario a £300-an-hour shrink would struggle to unravel, let alone a naïve, frightened 21-year-old!

Future stories will delve deep into all Troy's relationships, as he desperately attempts to come to terms with his new identity as a decidedly reluctant Antichrist. His journey is set to take him back to Hell, all the way up to Heaven and even on to the mean streets of Camden, North London, where a whole host of weirdness awaits. Hopefully, you'll be along for the ride.

The current plan is to release **Devilchild** Volume II at some point next year (maybe even in time for Comics 2003).

The format will be similar to this volume with one fairly lengthy story plus four or five shorter strips. We're now on the look out for artists interested in contributing so why not send some samples to the address elsewhere on this page? We'd love to hear from you.

By the way, anyone thinking about publishing a comic or graphic novel should give **www.blambot.com** a look. As well as featuring loads of information on how to put out your own comic, the site contains a number of fonts, which are **free** to download for non-profit-making self-publishers everywhere. We've made use of several of their free fonts in this volume and simply can't recommend them highly enough.

In closing, I'd just like to thank all four of the artists who worked so hard to bring my oft confusing panel descriptions and overwritten dialogue to such energetic, beautifully rendered life in this volume. Tim Doe, Peet Clack, Tim Twelves take a bow. Deserving extra special praise, though, is Natalie Sandells, whose professionalism, dedication and talent has made this first release such a total pleasure to work on. The girl's a fucking superstar.

Finally, we want to know what you think about this first volume, so why not drop us a line? Or, if you'd like to show your loyalty and admiration for **Devilchild** in a more demonstrative way, we have a range of fine cotton t-shirts for sale on page 79.

Let's push things forward.

Andy Winter
Darkest Essex
April 2002

In **Devilchild** Volume II: Troy's depressed, Satan reckons he's got Hell's election in the bag, and Beatrice, Lucia and Witch Rhea are drunk and in trouble up to their necks. '**Heavier Than Heaven**' is written and lettered by **Andy Winter** and illustrated by **Natalie Sandells**.

THURSDAY, 7:30PM
HERMES APARTMENTS, KENSINGTON, WEST LONDON...

WHERE TO TONIGHT, MISS JOCASTA?

VELOCITY GIRL

"A Night On The Town"

Writer: Andrew Winter
Art & Letters: Tim Twelves

I THINK *SUGAR REEF* FOR DINNER WITH NATS AND TOBY, FOLLOWED BY DRINKS AND DANCING MY FABULOUS ARSE OFF AT *TOKYO JOE'S*, *RED CUBE*, AND MAYBE WIND UP AT *CHINA WHITE*. NOW I'M RUNNING A LITTLE LATE, SO BE A DEAR *AND GET THE BLOODY LEAD OUT!*

...YOUR MOST DECADENT FANTASY?

HMM... HOW ABOUT BLOWING TWO GRAND ON A BOTTLE OF KRUG... *AND THEN TIPPING IT OVER A TRAMP!*

OR MUNCHING BELUGA CAVIAR OUT OF A YOUNG IVANA TRUMP'S AS...

UMMM.. THANKS TOBY... I THINK THAT'S ENOUGH!

8:15PM

I'M A TOTAL FAN! CAN I HAVE YOUR AUTOGRAPH?

10:35PM

12:27AM

SURE, I'D BE HONOURED!

11:06PM

SSNNNFF

12:08AM

CAN YOU WRITE 'TO GRAHAM, WITH LOVE'?

I THINK I CAN DO BETTER THAN THAT...

Feathers

Writer: Andy Winter
Artist: Tim Doe

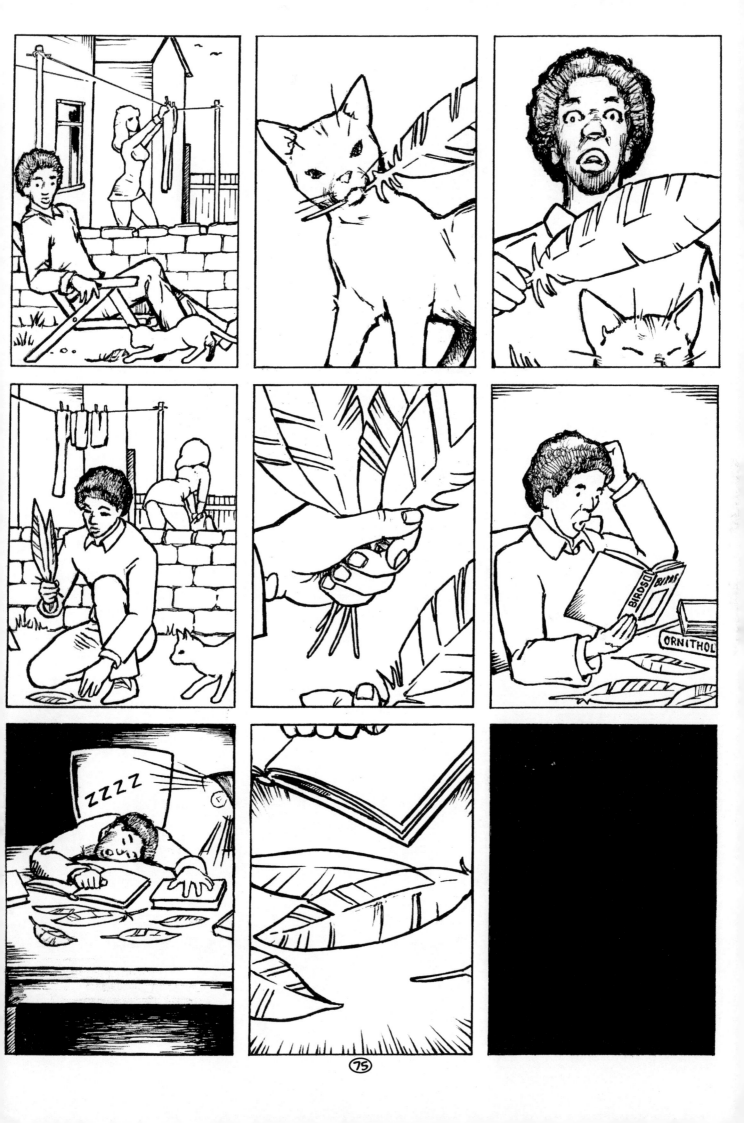

Dear Mr. Llewellyn,

Many thanks for bringing the feathers you found in your garden for identification

Although it didn't take us long to deduce which species they were from, we were somewhat surprised all the same.

It appears that you have recently been visited by an osprey — a female most likely

In the UK these birds are found only in Scotland, and even there their numbers are very small

To find a specimen this far south is extraordinary and in my experience quite unprecedented

It is therefore likely that the bird in question has escaped from a zoo or private collection

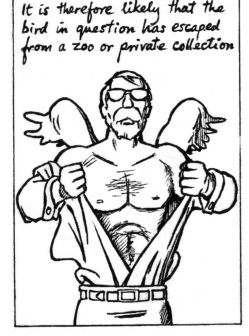

Hopefully this satisfactorily answers all your questions

Yours sincerely, Elmer Dinkley (Bird Division Curator, Natural History Museum)

THE END

LOOK DASHINGLY DEVILISH IN A DEVILCHILD T-SHIRT!

YOU'VE BOUGHT THE DEVILCHILD GRAPHIC NOVEL, NOW BECOME THE ENVY OF ALL YOUR MATES BY MODELLING A DASHING BUT DASTARDLY DEVILCHILD T-SHIRT!

EACH SHIRT COSTS £8 (P&P £1 FOR ONE SHIRT, 80p FOR EACH ADDITIONAL ITEM). PLEASE ENQUIRE FOR PRICES IN EUROS AND U.S. DOLLARS.

ALL SHIRTS ARE 100% PRE-SHRUNK COTTON AND ARE CURRENTLY AVAILABLE IN XL ONLY.

SIMPLY PHOTOCOPY THE ORDER FORM BELOW AND SEND IT TO: ANDY WINTER (MOONFACE PRESS), P.O. BOX 5593, SOUTHEND-ON-SEA, ESSEX, SS1 2WY. CHEQUES (WITH CHEQUE GUARANTEE CARD NUMBER ON THE BACK) AND POSTAL ORDERS SHOULD BE MADE OUT TO ANDY WINTER.

D001

D002

D003

Name		
Address		
	Postcode	
Email		

Please send me (write quantity in box):

D001 ☐ @ £8 each   Amount £_____

D002 ☐ @ £8 each   Amount £_____

D003 ☐ @ £8 each   Amount £_____

P&P   £_____

TOTAL   £_____

EARTH 2302: THE HOUSES OF PARLIAMENT — HOME TO WOULD-BE GALACTIC TYRANT, *BLOAK THE BADAZZ*.

YOUR REIGN OF *TERROR* ENDS HERE, BLOAK.

Rarggghhh!

What the druck?!

WE'VE *SUCCEEDED*. BLOAK THE BADAZZ IS DEAD AND HISTORY IS *REWRITTEN!*

WHATEVER. CAN WE GO *HOME* NOW, MY FEET ACHE?

DON'T YOU *REALISE* WHAT WE'VE JUST *ACCOMPLISHED*, YOU PUMPED UP *PRIMA DONNA?*

BIG BRAIN, BIG MOUTH, *SMALL DICK!*

SHUT UP, YOU STEROID-PACKED STRUMPET.

YOU'VE BEEN IN A ROTTEN MOOD FOR DAYS, AND I'M *SICK* OF IT!

DOSH AND PECS DO TIME TRAVEL

WRITER/LETTERER: ANDY WINTER ARTIST: PEET!

EARTH 3002: THE SANCTUARY, HOME TO THE PLANET'S MOST FAMOUS *CELEBRITY* COUPLE: TRILLIONAIRE INVENTOR, *DAVID DOSH*, AND HIS BODY BUILDING WIFE, *PRISCILLA PECS*.

JEEZ, HASN'T THIS *TIME MACHINE* STUFF BEEN DONE TO DEATH? IT'S *SO* 20TH CENTURY.

CAN PRISCILLA SHOW A BIT MORE *CLEAVAGE?*

¡○(○(○

AREN'T YOU *MEDDLING* WITH THE NATURAL ORDER OF THINGS?

CAN I GO BACK IN TIME TO MAKE SURE I *NEVER* MEET MY WIFE?

IS IT *TRUE* THE DESCENDANTS OF H.G. WELLS MIGHT *SUE?*

HOW'S YOUR *FOOT*, DAVID?

ALL YOUR QUESTIONS WILL BE ANSWERED IN DUE COURSE, BUT NOW WE *MUST* CONCENTRATE ON THE *MISSION* AT HAND.

WHEN I INVENTED THIS *CHRONAL NAVIGATOR* - OR TIME MACHINE - I DID SO WITH ONLY *ONE* THING IN *MIND*.

AND THAT NOBLE PURPOSE WAS TO BRING PEACE, TRANQUILITY AND JUSTICE TO THE PEOPLE OF THE 31ST CENTURY.

OH *PUH-LEESE!*

TODAY I PLAN TO TRAVEL BACK IN TIME TO THE *24TH CENTURY* AND THERE RID EARTH'S HISTORY OF IT'S *GREATEST* SHAME.

IN SHORT, I PLAN TO *KILL BLOAK THE BADAZZ!*

STUNNED SILENCE!

BLOAK'S REIGN OF *TERROR* 700 YEARS AGO IS THE MAIN REASON FOR *EARTH'S* MANY *ILLS* TODAY.

BECAUSE OF HIM NO-ONE IN THE KNOWN UNIVERSE WILL TRADE WITH US, BECAUSE OF HIM HUMANS ARE *REVILED* ALL THE WAY FROM *LE SAUX* TO THE *LAMPA'RD* SECTOR.

IT IS MY *DESTINY* TO *CHANGE* ALL THAT - AND BY *PRESCOTT'S PURPLE PARROT,* CHANGE IT I *WILL!*

YAHOO!

WE *LOVE* YOU, DAVID!

GO DOSH!

81

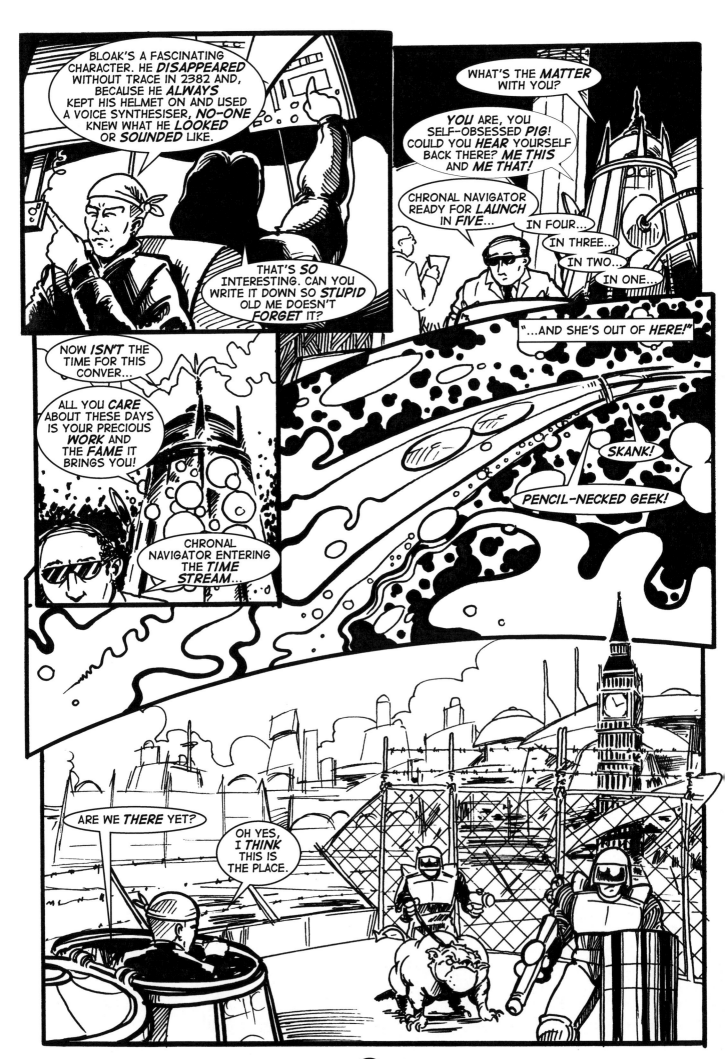

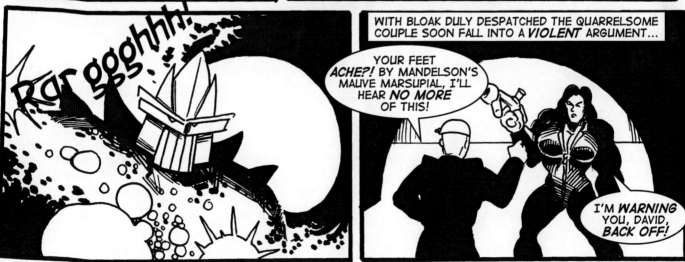